This book belongs to

Leah Matexe

For my sons Ethan and Alasdair, and my daughter
Lauren, who all love funny stories - L.S.

First Published in Great Britain in 2021

Text copyright © Lauren Swan, 2021
(laurenswanauthor.com)
Illustrations copyright © Lauren Swan, 2021

A Lonely Little Castle

Written by Lauren Swan
Illustrated by Monika Suska

A **lonely** little castle,
sitting on a hill.
Cold and dark and empty,
quiet and so still.

Along came a little ghost
who had a peek inside.
"What a perfect place to live
for someone who has died!"

A CREEPY little castle,
sitting on a hill.
Cold and dark and
haunted,
quiet and so still.

Passing in her carriage,
a princess stopped to see.
"How quaint! This will be splendid
with a touch of TLC."

"Yes, this shall do nicely.
I'll get some peace, no doubt.
But first I'd better dig a moat to keep
the rabble out!"

A **pretty** little castle,
surrounded by a moat.
Lived in by a princess
and a slightly angry ghost.

The sound of running water
brought a troll out of the wood,
searching for a place to build...

"This river looks quite good!"

A charming little castle, where now there is a troll,
living underneath a bridge and charging quite a toll.

A little while later,
a goat came trotting past,
looking for a bridge to cross
to find some greener grass.

The goat was followed closely
by a wolf who seemed quite wry.
"An angry woodsman's after me!
I've no idea why!"

A **BUSY** little castle, with a happy munching goat.
Exploited by a troll, and surrounded by a moat.

Shared by a spirit and a very cross princess, who all now have to put up with a wolf who wears a dress.

A knight rode up upon the scene,
and through the door he strode.
"Nice place! I think I'll stay a while,
I'm weary from the road."

And who should come behind him,
later that same day?
But a pesky, ugly dragon
that the knight forgot to slay.

The dragon toured the home and said, "This place will be just right!
It comes ready with a damsel, and a knight I'd like to fight!"

A **crowded** little castle,
where space is getting tight.
With a wolf, and a dragon,
and a princess, and a knight.

Haunted by a spirit,
and grazed on by a goat.
With a troll under a bridge
that runs across a moat.

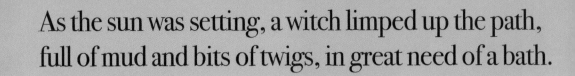

As the sun was setting, a witch limped up the path,
full of mud and bits of twigs, in great need of a bath.

"I need to stay the night," she said.
"I got knocked off my broom,
by the biggest brute you've ever seen!
I'll take the top floor room."

"Have you got a messenger?
Can someone fetch a nurse?
Being over twelve feet tall
really is a curse!"

"I was minding my own
    business,
just gazing at the sky,
when a woman riding on a twig
    flew right into my eye."

A **noisy** little castle, with a witch having a bath, and a princess in the tower, who can't contain her wrath.

A giant being bandaged, and a ghost who's in a huff, and a nosy wolf who's rifling through other people's stuff.

A knight fighting a dragon over who will get the bed, and a troll forever listening for footsteps overhead.

A goat who eats the grass that grows upon the ridge of the hill under the castle, with the moat that has a bridge.

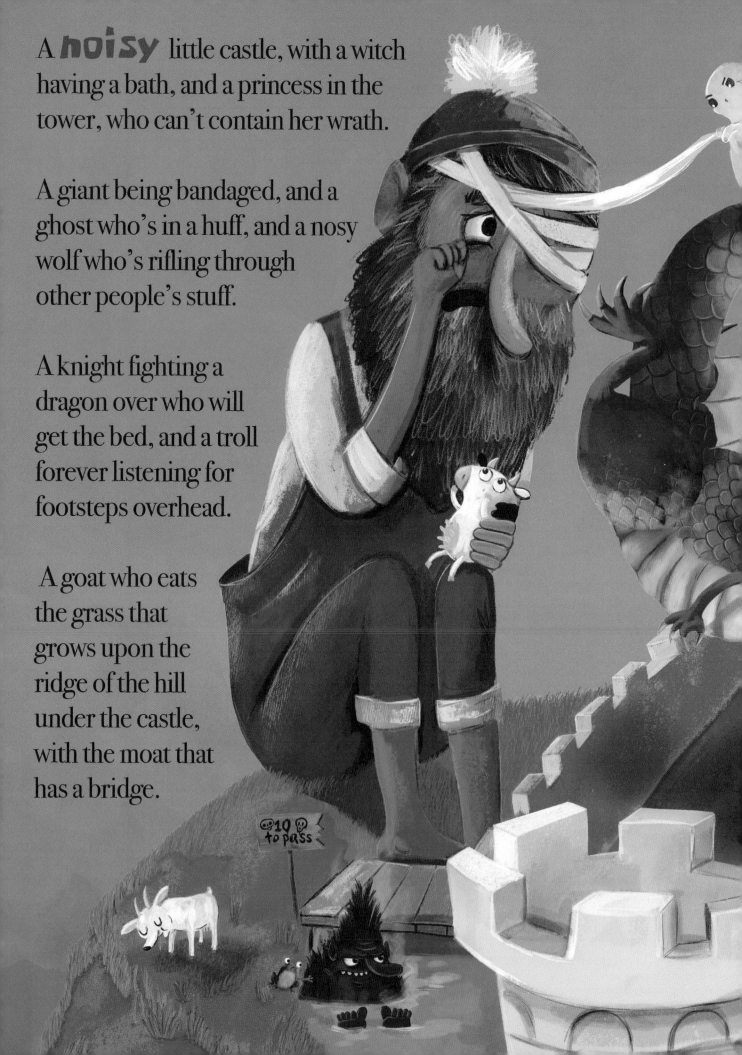

10 to pass

The princess threw a tantrum.
"This castle's overthrown!
I will not live with riffraff!
I'm off, I'm going home!"

The dragon followed shortly
since there was no girl to guard...

And the knight no longer wished to stay; his room was burnt and charred.

After wasting the hot water,
and draining half the moat,

the witch packed up her broken broom
and rode off on the goat.

The giant, feeling better,
decided to depart.

But as he stepped upon the bridge
it cracked and fell apart.

A lonely little castle,
with only one at home…

A ghost who's thrilled to finally
be living all alone.